THE DESERT OF LOP

Also by Raoul Schrott

Finis terrae: ein Nachlass (1995)

Hotels (1995)

Die Erfindung der Poesie: Gedichte
aus den ersten viertausend Jahren (1997)

Die Musen: Fragmente einer
Sprache der Dichtung (1997)

Fragmente einer Sprache der Dichtung:
Grazer Poetikvorlesung (1997)

Tropen: über das Erhabene (1998)

Bakchen: nach Euripides (1999)

Das Geschlecht der Engel, der Himmel der Heiligen:
ein Brevier (2001)

Gilgamesh: Epos (2001)

Khamsin (2002)

THE DESERT OF LOP

Raoul Schrott

Translated from the German by

KAREN LEEDER

PICADOR

First published 2004 by Picador
an imprint of Pan Macmillan Ltd
Pan Macmillan, 20 New Wharf Road, London N1 9RR
Basingstoke and Oxford
Associated companies throughout the world
www.panmacmillan.com

ISBN 0 330 49153 9

1 3 5 7 9 8 6 4 2

A CIP catalogue record for this book is available from
the British Library.

Typeset by Macmillan Text Department
Printed and bound in Great Britain by
Mackays of Chatham plc, Chatham, Kent

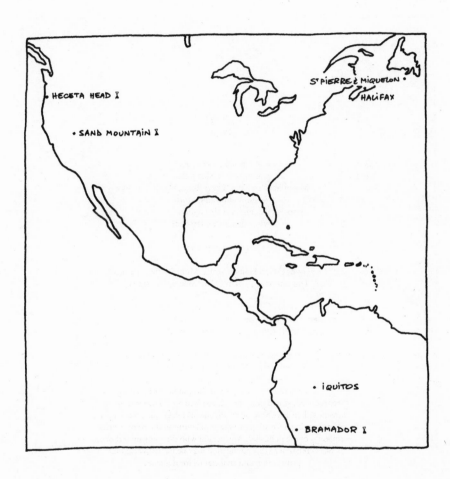

I

In the middle of a cornfield close to the Japanese town of Nima stands a glass pyramid. Inside is to be found the largest sandglass in the world.

Each New Year at midnight the dignitaries of the town gather to turn it over; it takes exactly a year for the upper bulb to empty, the lower one to fill.

II

The house stands on a hill. He has rented the upper storey; a staircase at the side of the house leads up to it.

In the single room there is an oak table and a chest; in the window alcove a pine cone, a greegree, and a stone.

This is all that reminds him of the three women who once shared his life.

His landlady sends her daughter up with his food; she sets it down on the table for him in a bowl.

His name is Raoul Louper; he is 43 years old, a wandering Jew on one side of the family, and was born on the island of Porquerolles in the Gulf of Toulon.

The village is not far from Alexandria.

The coast falls away uniformly into the sea.

III

The girl tells her mother that this man who goes by the name of Louper always seems to be looking over her shoulder, not so much ignoring her, but as if there were someone else standing behind her.

He has black, bushy eyebrows and two deep furrows in his forehead. For a man he is small and scarcely reaches up to her chin; that is what she sees.

Raoul caught her once opening the chest. Inside were three dozen little glasses and bottles filled with all colours of sand, white, black,

and every shade of red.

He never said a word about it.

During the day he seldom leaves the house.

In the evenings he joins the men sitting in the cafe. The women cross the street and enter their houses. Under the hijab, their faces can scarcely be seen.

IV

Raoul has only travelled to the Siwa Oasis in the south twice before. The road is
perfectly straight and covered with asphalt; it leads across the plain, where the basin of
Siwa suddenly opens up before it. In winter the basin fills with water and reflects the
mountains behind it as far as the horizon.
In the north, travelling on foot, one has to stick to the road. To left and right the new
two-lane highway is lined with barbed wire.
There are signs warning of minefields.
When a house is built here, a lorry arrives and unloads rubble from the quarries onto the
plot. The house Raoul is living in could only be built after a herd of donkeys had been
driven up the hill.

V

The woman he will love one day has green eyes and red hair. Between her legs it is paler, but thick towards her belly, like the throat of a fox.

VI

Once a week Raoul catches the bus to Cairo. From the museum one walks up the street, then takes the second turning on the left, through a garden and a wrought-iron gate. Odoric of Pordonone himself had passed through a valley not far from the River of Joy. The Franciscan monk had seen the many corpses scattered around and heard the sinister noise of the Nacars, which gripped him with terror. Now: this valley is seven or eight miles long. And he had been warned; if an infidel were to enter it, he would certainly perish.

He, however, did not hesitate, says Török, and looks up from his reading with a pause. The Hungarian Professor is holding the pages of the itinerarium at the very edges between his finger and thumb.

On the rock on one side of the valley was the face of a huge and terrible man: it was so terrible that his soul almost died away within him. And he crossed himself . . .

He scrambled up onto a mountain of sand and looked around him again and again; but there was no one to be seen; he heard only the loud but marvellous drumming on the Nacars. The ridge above him glittered in the light; silver was scattered everywhere like splinters of slate. A little of this treasure he scooped up and hid under his shirt. But then he was overcome with the fear that all hope of return was in vain, and he flung the silver as far from him as he could.

It is the month of Ramadan; the bus would not be leaving until after sunset, around midnight, or maybe not at all.

VII

Near Grosseto on the Mediterranean Sea there is a little bay called Cala Violina. Raoul had discovered the name by chance; that was years ago, years he now counts on the fingers of both hands.

There he also met his first wife.

No, she had met him.

He had been strolling up and down the beach in the evening when the other bathers were already packing up their towels and umbrellas. He glanced neither to right nor left, but this doesn't mean that he was inconspicuous.

She was as taut and lithe as a country woman. As she swam along she would dive down, flicking her bottom up out of the water a little. When her head emerged above the waves, she would snort loudly.

Raoul had always been mistaken about bodies.

Lying inside her, it was soft and easy to reach her; but although she tensed her body he still found nothing to hold on to. Even so, it was easy to get used to it.

He stayed with her that whole summer, selling slices of coconut and cans of Coke from a bin of ice on the beach. That's how he kept his head above water.

Then a letter arrived from a man called Shigeo, telling him that there was a bay not far from him with the name Kotohiki; Koto means 'harp'.

He saw out the rest of the winter by getting up early every morning to help out at the baker's, and by spring he had saved enough to go to Japan.

VIII

It was not that long ago that the Hungarian Professor and I went to pick up Raoul, then
the three of us drove on together down to Siwa.

At the conference there, to which delegates from America, Italy, and Japan had also been
invited, there was much talk of a humming, howling, and groaning
that would get louder and then fade again.

The discussion moved on to a curious rumbling from the sea, the fog guns on the
Belgian coast, and the so-called Guns of Barisal.

The sound of a foghorn was described, thunder.

A lorry that made the building shake.

Telephone wires singing even though the wind was still.

Which are the sounds that have existed
since the very beginning
of the world and which of them still sound as they did then? asked someone in a break
between all the lectures.

In the evening, although it was already dark, we were shown the ruins of the palace on
the summit by torchlight. A little further down there was an artesian well. The water was
a deep shade of green, the green of the plants and algae in it. In the torchlight we could
see the bubbles coming up and the clouds of steam. If you are weary and want to freshen
up, the best thing is to wash your feet, said Raoul.

It had been the Chief of Police who showed us round in Siwa. Alexander the Great, he
explained, came here to consult the oracle. In Delphi, he continued with a learned air,
earth was used to make prophecies, it was water in Delos, in Pisa fire, and in the
Dordogne air.

He means Dodona, I whispered, turning to Török. In Siwa we use all of them, the Police
Chief insisted, undaunted.

IX

In order to buy his passage back from Japan, Raoul Louper had signed up to work in the galley of a container ship for the ship's cook. They docked in Port Moresby, in Singapore, Aden, Port Saïd, Alexandria, and finally Venice; the voyage lasted two months.

At the harbour Francesca had been waiting. On the train to Grosseto there had been too many people in the compartment for them to speak freely. They passed an aqueduct; in the window the sun went down in a milky haze. Raoul remembers it, as if it were yesterday.

On the way home from the station, he insisted on taking the detour leading down to the bay before anything else. At the spot where the track pitched off into the ravine stood a single pine tree. That was where she finally forced herself to say it.

A pine cone passed from one hand to the other.

She had always had several lovers at the same time: she had never been able to make up her mind. But to him she had been faithful longer than to anyone else.

He stayed on in her flat for a while. The sudden absence of feeling between them was easier to bear than not knowing where to go. Nevertheless they continued sharing the little bathroom in the mornings.

The freckles on her neck, Raoul can see them as if it were today.

X

On one of the previous weekends they had taken the Professor's battered old Peugeot
and made a trip to Sinai. They were stopped several times on the way at police
checkpoints. Of the freighters on the Suez Canal only the upper decks and masts were
visible protruding above the raised bank.

Further south, just a few kilometres inland from the coast, lies Jebel Nakus; a huge dune
has grown up against it. The peculiar rushing noise sometimes audible in its vicinity at
first made German travellers in the year 1810 think of
an aeolian harp.

But the name 'Nakus' comes from the flat discs of wood that were kept in front of
chapels by the Desert Fathers in Egypt; they would beat them to call the monks to
prayer. The beating of these gongs reminded the Arabs of their Nacars, giant clams,
which they used for a similar purpose. Thus, after Christianity had been forbidden, the
legend arose of a monastery buried at the foot
of the mountain.

If one walks up to the ridge today one can see how the erosion of the rock is causing the
sand to be constantly built up in heaps. It begins with a gentle rustling, then a murmuring
that at last becomes deafening, as deafening as an endless salvo of cannon-fire.

XI

An aeolian harp, says Török, the Hungarian Professor, is something which makes the
world audible.
From the branches of the oak tree in Dodona people would suspend stones, mussel shells,
or little figurines of clay, close enough that they would clatter gently against each other.
How else can the wind possibly be heard?
It would be nothing, not even a rustling: it would simply be wind.
But in this way the things knock against each other and once in a while a kind
of harmony arises.
What else could this have been but harmony with god?
And what about earth or fire? objects Raoul.
In the fire one sees faces.

XII

Osodani is located on a Japanese island.

Above the waterline the bank turns a loamy brown colour, but its edges are made of pure quartz; salt dries into white streaks, mother of pearl shimmering in the sunlight. Each wave that breaks takes up a little sand; then gives it back again.

The rasp of footsteps as one walks along the beach has been likened to many things, even to the croaking of bullfrogs.

XIII

The syllable of sand, the sibilants of the wind.

Sand in Arabic is called *r'ml*, in Japanese it is *suna*, *sha* in Chinese, *arena* in Spanish, *areia* in Portuguese, in Kenya, Zaire, and Rwanda it goes by the name *muchanga*, in Chad it is *nangue*, pronounced as in the French, and in Russian they say *pesok*. In Burkina Faso it is called *tchintchin*.

XIV

In the cafe he is left in peace. One sees one's own loneliness reflected in the faces of others.

Raoul drinks his tea, chews the mint leaves, then the pine nuts, rolls himself a cigarette. When one is alone, one should make such things last a long time, so as to appear busy.

He is quite clumsy with his hands, but he lays the tobacco out carefully, rolls it back and forth with his fingers, then stretches the paper and licks it, hoping that it will stick.

It is important to have something to fix one's eyes upon, to stop them wandering up to the women standing at their windows.

If someone joins him at his table, in spite of all his efforts, he has only one topic of conversation.

XV

The second one, he had seen for the first time as she pushed her way to the bar and rested her hand on his shoulder, as if it was perfectly natural.

There was jazz being played in the bar. Raoul did not much like music; it had too many notes for his taste.

Later when the bar was packed, he went to stand outside at the entrance. The sky was the colour of the neon streetlamps.

She had come in a sailing boat; he guessed that from the way she said 'sea dog' in English and wore plimsolls. Her hair was black. It fell to her shoulders; on her forehead though it was cut short.

Absentmindedly she drew it up in her hands; it was scarcely long enough for a ponytail. Then she started rummaging in the pocket of her jeans. He gave her the elastic band he had been fiddling with the whole time.

It was in a different town.

Besides, she was called Arlette.

XVI

On the old Silk Road, in the province of Sinjiang, says Török, who has found another quotation, another itinerarium, there are caves full of paintings and a rock face with a figure of Buddha carved into it almost eight storeys high. On top of the cliff stands a pagoda, and next to it a sacred site, the Temple of Thunder; beyond that the desert begins once more.

To the left of the path, further toward the oasis of Dun Huang, at the foot of the Ming Sha Shan dunes, lies a small lake. There a Chinese general and his army had once set up camp on their march westwards.

In the middle of the night they were taken unawares by the enemy. The general ordered that the drums be sounded to warn his troops and call them to arms, but no sooner had the battle begun than a sandstorm whipped up, fell from the mountain, and buried the two armies.

If the wind blows across the ridge of the dunes, it is said that one can hear the drumming still.

XVII

Tell me a story, Arlette had said. What is the most beautiful story you know? Make one up for me, no matter whether it is true.

XVIII

There was once a Public Writer in Dun Huang, who had a daughter, named Crescent Moon. One day, in the market, between the oranges, dates, tomatoes, and coriander, she met a young painter called Sha-shan-ze. She had filled her basket with vegetables and fruit for a feast that her father was holding that evening.

However, in the middle of the night a terrible storm blew up and scattered the guests far, far and wide; but it brought Crescent Moon and Sha-shan-ze together. The young painter saved her life and she gave him a lock of her hair in gratitude.

Sha-shan-ze went on his way and it would be ten years before they saw one another again. The girl had grown up to be beautiful and the painter had found work in the caves, where he was commissioned to paint frescoes, so that there could be a thousand Buddhas.

One day Crescent Moon and her father visited the caves to pray. It was the lock of hair that he wore around his neck that revealed the painter to Crescent Moon; she fell in love and asked him to marry her.

Her father, the Public Writer, however, refused to give his blessing to such a marriage: the painter was completely penniless, he told her, and nothing and no one could persuade him to give his consent. From that moment on Crescent Moon would come evening after evening to the Caves of the Thousand Buddhas, under the pretext of wanting to pray. And the frescoes become more and more beautiful; on each and every face it was her eyes, her nose, her mouth.

When the Public Writer got wind of their ruse, he ordered Crescent Moon to be locked in her room. And he made it clear to her that there was only one man she would marry: a general.

Sha-shan-ze died of a broken heart when he heard what had happened. But before he drew his last breath he asked to be buried alongside the path leading to the Caves of the Thousand Buddhas.

Over the mound of his grave a dune of sand formed. Coming from within one could hear on some nights a muffled pounding, like that of a broken heart.

Crescent Moon knew nothing of the painter's death. To make her more compliant, her father pretended that she might perhaps marry the painter one day after all; and the General courted her with his daily visits. But the time came when she ran out of excuses to forestall him further, and in the end she came to believe that Sha-shan-ze had forgotten her.

However, when the day finally came to be carried in a sedan chair to the wedding ceremony, they happened to pass by the dune, whose faint beating could be heard deep within.

Crescent Moon listened in secret as the bearers recounted the sad story, but no words were needed; she had recognized the heartbeat all along.

Beside herself with misery, she jumped down out of the sedan chair and ran to the dune sobbing bitterly. Her tears ran down to form a trickle of water, and the rivulet swelled to be a stream, only to pour into the lake; she cried so hard that nothing could quiet her tears, and she died on the grave of her beloved.

That is how it came to pass that the two of them were united for all eternity and the crescent of the lake came to lie at the foot of the dune.

XIX

In Quimper, Raoul had found himself work on a trawler that fished the seas of
Newfoundland, out of St Pierre and Miquelon. The work was hard but well paid.
Icebergs drifted to the south.
They sailed into a storm for three weeks and had thirty kilos of cannabis on board.
Sometimes there were scuffles.
Close to the coast they dragged a beam along the seabed to stun the fish, so they could
catch them in the net trailing behind.
That was strictly prohibited, but no one gave a damn.
Once they found a frozen chicken in the nets still frozen solid.

XX

In Halifax he collected his pay.

The rocky coast was flat and black; across the marshes were swathes of white cotton grass, the land a looming blue shadow. He hired a car and drove via Montreal and the Great Lakes to Chicago and then on, only stopping to sleep at a Motel Six.

In Salt Lake City he went into a shop and bought himself a pair of cowboy boots, like the ones he had dreamed of as a boy. His instep was too high; he could only slip them on with a plastic bag over his foot.

The first night he slept with his boots on because he could not get them off on his own.

XXI

Then one morning Raoul had found himself standing in front of the lighthouse at Heceta
Head, Oregon, and had finally seen the Pacific from the other side.
There, at Ten Mile Creek and Cannon Beach, he walked the dunes one by one; he took
his time, slept in the back of the car, and washed himself in the public toilets.
It does not only depend on the type of sand, but also on the weather, the wind, and
the humidity.
The attendant who had worked there for exactly twenty-one years said he knew nothing
about any noises of the kind Raoul described; and anyway the beach buggies
wrecked everything.

XXII

Twenty-two miles east of Fallon, Nevada, there are two crescent-shaped dunes. A stony path leads down to the grassland at the foot of them. They are over one hundred metres high and marked on the map as 'Sand Mountain'.

If you walk down the steeper leeward side, there is a noise like a low-flying bomber, or one of the fighter planes from the Second World War that are the pride and joy of various flying clubs.

Raoul took back a handful of sand for Arlette from there too.

Very few people think of something like that.

And he sent her a postcard, on the front of which he drew a heart; but he arrived before the postman had delivered it.

XXIII

Arlette, Arlette, Arlette! She had strong opinions, political ones.

In Quimper you can still see a sign which says 'It is Forbidden to Spit on the Ground and speak Breton'. It used to hang on a wall in the street, but now it hung in the restaurant where Arlette worked as a waitress.

When the fishing fleet did not go out, and there was no work to be had in the fish factory, Raoul Louper stayed with her. Her father had bought a little place for her. Raoul cooked and kept house. She always came back late from work.

One of the things they argued about was the door. It had to be either open or closed; one of them could open it, the other close it; but both used the same handle. In that way, or so Raoul reckoned, neither would have the upper hand.

The same could be said for many other things.

Such things are not important, but had become ever more so.

XXIV

Once a year Francesca phoned, mostly when she had found herself a new lover. They got along better and better. Just as she was about to hang up Francesca would always say how much she missed him.

It seems that women only ever missed Raoul Louper after he had left.

XXV

The first time he went walking with Arlette he noticed that she limped every so often, as if one leg was shorter than the other.

The first time he slipped his hand under her pullover, he felt breasts that seemed enormous to him (that he had little experience excuses nothing); her hips though were as narrow as a boy's, and she had tiny feet like those of a child.

The first time he slept with her, he felt sick when he awoke. After that it always took time for Raoul to get used to her again; that he came straight from the ship helped.

He had always been mistaken about women.

And yet, both of them left the light on.

XXVI

When she got out of bed she always covered herself up. When they slept together, she could only climax when she was sitting astride him and he watched as she made herself come. She went at it roughly as if she could only feel one half of her body.

His own body he didn't particularly like either, his belly, hands, toes. These are not things one likes to mention.

Nor that she had lost her virginity to the father of the Italian family where she had worked for the summer as an au pair. Once a week he went to the barber, said Arlette; he would come back with his sideburns trimmed to the millimetre and his cheeks red with aftershave.

Her skin smelled of lentils.

XXVII

Every time he came into port on the trawler, she would be waiting there for him in her dark sunglasses. Behind them, her eyes were blue. Raoul liked nothing better than to take off her glasses and stare into that deep blue, which was dark, darker than the sea. Love: he tried to imitate it but he failed, time and again. And the weight of Arlette's breasts never stopped confusing him (that might seem ridiculous, unless one knows what it means).

In the darkness of their bedroom he sometimes watched the moon come up, framed by the window, white like all happiness. Raoul said it in French, where it rhymes: *lune* and *fortune*.

XXVIII

He poured the sand he had brought back for her into a glass bowl in the kitchen – a fist deep. Then he stuck an iron rod into the pile of sand. There was a grinding, a rubbing and then, if one listened carefully, something that sounded distantly like a dog barking, somewhere behind the houses.

XXIX

Török has his theories.

The phenomenon of a singing dune, he explains, is most often to be observed on its slip-face. And it seems to have something to do with the dull, rounded shape of the grains of sand.

It is the wind that blunts them. It scatters them; lifting them, so that they fly up, ricocheting off the ground, whirling other grains up into the air, rubbing away at each other and thereby losing their edges. For this they have to be carried over long distances; but it is also the friction inside the dune that leaves them polished so smoothly.

The Kelso Dunes in California are 29 km from the coast; the Kauai and Niihau Dunes on Hawaii only 290 m. From Jebel Nakus to the Red Sea the odometer registered exactly 2.9 km.

How far away is Ming Sha Shan? Török wants to know now.

In America the top of a pine tree just protrudes from one of the dunes,

in Africa the sand has covered the asphalt,

in Asia it has buried telephone masts.

XXX

On the other hand, expounds Török, it is known that the grains of sand in the
Korizo Dunes in Libya and in the Egyptian Gilf Kebir are quite different sizes.
At the Sand Mountain in Nevada, or in the Kalahari for that matter, the sand is not even
remotely spherical. And the Dune of Ming Sha Shan is made up entirely of quartz; under
the microscope the grains are scarred and cratered, like moons or meteorites.
Or perhaps it depends on the humidity.
Or on a thin spherical layer binding them together.
Or . . .
But what does this explain? Or show in the end?
Even if you try with common table salt, Raoul interrupts, it will still work.
But now it is Török who is unwilling to concede, as the salt granules are angular,
resembling tiny cubes.
What one knows for sure, one must always be able to prove in another language, with
other words. But in that, it seems to me, Raoul never took much interest.

XXXI

In the Gilf Kebir I once saw time. It was a kind of wheat grass, its panicle bent down. In the morning a breeze came from the rising sun, and in the evening from where it set. Moved by the wind, the stalk traced a complete circle in the sand, like a clock which knows no hours.

XXXII

In Raoul Louper's love for Arlette there was always something that was still waiting to change shape. It was like one of the drawings of a Necker cube that one finds in magazines sometimes; its upper edges can only be held in the foreground if one concentrates hard.

He sometimes looked at Arlette absent-mindedly. She did not know what to make of it; she thought when he looked at her it was always with questions.

Raoul avoided giving an answer; there are some things one does not say to a woman if one wants to love her.

When Arlette lay on the sofa, her legs hanging over the arm, he stroked her toes with his fingers in passing; that made up for a lot of things. Nevertheless Raoul kept looking for something which would transform her for him.

In love, Raoul persuaded himself, there are always empty spaces, blind corners one can't see into, something that one has to fill out oneself.

One puts something in to make it all seem whole.

Why, as he is speaking now, does the word 'crystal' suddenly come to mind? Perhaps because love should be preserved; but that reminds him too much of the horoscopes Arlette was so fond of.

Something must remain undecided; that was a phrase she quoted at every opportunity: *quelque chose doit rester indécis.*

That's why he brought her the greegree.

XXXIII

Thursday evening in Cairo. The clouds like a horse's tail across the sky; the sun rolling
down the croup, along over the dome of the mosque and into the Nile.

Török lives with an Egyptian woman; they are happy together and often invite Raoul to
supper, sometimes with me too. Raoul doesn't enjoy going, they know that; but the
evenings turn out pleasantly enough for everyone in the end.

The first few times they only started discussing the sand after Török's wife had
gone to bed.

Now they are sitting late over their meal. The table-top is a mosaic of tiles, black and
white squares like a chessboard; the glasses like the pieces.

By the open window there is a eucalyptus tree.

The lampshade is orange.

XXXIV

The wind carries the grains of sand across the crest of the dunes; that is how they
become a slope, says Török, to begin at the beginning again.

At a certain point though the dune breaks. Then large fields of sand form and slip off
like avalanches. Like a snow-slab the layer nearer the top glides down over the slower one
beneath; they slip into each other and shear away.

Török's wife sets a bowl of fruit salad down on the table. She has made it with avocado,
cucumber, paprika and mango. In the Antarctic . . . says Török, but chokes and has to
reach for a glass of water. His mouth is stinging, but that won't stop him.

Raoul gradually becomes impatient.

In the Antarctic, he resumes, there are fields of dunes that run alongside each other in an
unbroken line for hundreds of kilometres, but are only a few metres high. One could
almost believe that they wander with the stormy winds blowing in those parts; but on the
TV false-colour images from the spy satellites there is no trace of them.

From the minaret the muezzin calls. There are crusts of bread and crumbs scattered on
the table between the empty plates. Török rolls them to and fro with his finger and round
the coffee-grinder.

He shares the opinion of the experts that these dunes are not caused by drifts of snow
brought by the wind, in the same way as dunes in the desert. It is known that there are
frozen streams beneath the surface of the ice, pushing towards the sea, but not where
their source lies.

XXXV

Algeria, that was El Oued, Touggourt, Ghardaia, El Golea, In Salah, and Tamanrasset; or the asphalt track to Quatre Chemins. It was winter; overnight a thin layer of ice formed in the water canisters, and when they woke the inside of their tents was coated with frost.

Raoul had an old Land-Rover; but the route one can take depends on the vehicles and travellers one might meet along the way. In Ghardaia he met two Germans who had decided quite suddenly one Christmas to head for the desert.

In the boot they had only a single canister of diesel, pliers, a screwdriver, and a parachute. One of them had himself hoisted up in the air, like they do with boats over water. When that put paid to the radiator they could only carry on with the heating turned right up.

Beyond Quatre Chemins they followed the old piste with its surface of reeds and clay to Gara Khanfoussa; a mountain that looks like a scarab from afar. It is surrounded by a ring of dunes still marked by the tracks of one of the Paris to Dakar rallies. The imprint of tyres remains visible in the sand for decades; once compressed, the grains are simply blown over it.

The Hungarian Professor pours another glass of the sour, local wine. I also once . . . but Raoul does not let him get a word in.

Everywhere there are petrol cans and tins of food lying around, scarcely rusted at all, and the piste crosses a plain where I found hundreds of arrowheads and hand axes.

One track ran right across a perfectly preserved grindstone; it had been broken clean in two.

The French call them *meules dormantes*, sleeping mills.

XXXVI

The Mercedes could not make it across the dunes. So Raoul made the trip to Erg
Tiffernine alone.

Tiffernine; he liked the name, maybe one day he would call his daughter that.

Climbing up, it is always two steps forward and one step back; they do not get any
higher, the dunes of the Sahara. At the foot they are the yellow of egg yolk, then grey
from the dust blown onto them, turning gradually purple towards the top, and finally
blood-red.

He took only water and a rucksack with him. He trusted the Germans to come looking
for him if the worst came to the worst, but though he doubted it privately, he preferred
not to think about it.

That was more than reckless.

The fear didn't disappear even as he walked; instead it grew with every step that took
him further from the Land-Rover.

From the ridge of the dunes you can look down into deep craters that have been swept
out by the wind right to the bleached rock beneath.

It was a different kind of time made visible.

One needed only to run one's hand through the sand to hear it. The sound was like that
of the deepest string of a cello or a double bass; just one single note, but lying in his
sleeping bag at night, it echoed on for over a quarter of an hour.

XXXVII

By the time they reached the military post at Amguid they were no longer on speaking terms. It had started with little things; the last orange. Or the tea, in the morning. It's not a question of being petty, but at some point enough is enough.

In Tamanrasset they finally parted without a word. In the throng of the market place, he had inadvertently driven over a box with his back wheel. It contained all the worldly goods of a Nigerian, who had bought it off someone from Mali, who in turn had it from somebody in Mauritania; but as a matter of fact it belonged to a trader from Nigeria. It was full of sunglasses; the tyre had only run over the left-hand lenses, but alas all of them.

A crowd gathered, and the palaver lasted hours.

And then what happened? asked the Hungarian Professor.

I paid, answered Raoul. Too much of course; but then the Nigerian did give me the greegree that he was wearing round his neck as a gift. As if I had bought his friendship with my money too.

Every greegree has the beginning of a Sura from the Koran sewn up inside it. Time and again I am tempted to slit the seam open and look, says Raoul, but in the end I never do. Perhaps that is what gives it its power.

XXXVIII

There are mountains there, a huge volcanic massif in the middle of the desert. Zodiacal light
and the Southern Cross.

He had risen at four o'clock in the morning and climbed the path up to the hermitage on
the Assekrem in darkness. For three hours nothing but the sun rose, the sun in the wind,
which froze on his skin, the sun in the night.

And for the first time a calmness came over him; something eased off, lifted from him.
The hermit who lived up there, and who had once been a baker in Marseille, was holding
a service in his hut; the altar was a slab of stone supported by three columns of basalt
and a goatskin spread out before it.

As long as he lives he will never convert anyone to anything, said Raoul; I don't believe
he really even wants to.

XXXIX

As soon as he returned from Algeria, Arlette told him she was going to leave him.
She gave no reason and also handed back the gift he had brought her.
His gifts always resembled one another.
Decisions are always arrived at during absences.
They hardly ever seem to have a cause, only a certain symbolism.

XL

When one love is over, it is time to change place. And should one ever return, it is always by chance. The town where one once lived will always remain the way it has stayed in one's memory. The fact that by then many things have become unrecognizable does not mean, however, that anything has really changed.

Raoul had gone back to Italy, to Grosseto, to the little bay called Cala Violina. Walking along the beach above the waterline, the sand rustles like a violin bow which has been rubbed with colophony, even if this has not been done for a long time.

Francesca took him in for a few days and through her he managed to find work in a hotel, in the kitchen there. A little bottle of turpentine appeared on the bedside table, to prevent the sheets from getting stained with tar.

The sands of the Scottish island of Eigg, as Mr Shigeo had informed him then, had also only recently lost their peculiar character; perhaps the newly built groyne had altered the pattern of the tides, or perhaps the many oil tankers were the cause.

Raoul wrote page after page to Arlette. Francesca told him it would be pointless and turned her attentions to others again. As she often made a lot of noise about it, he took himself off for long walks.

XLI

The chef there was from Naples; he had dreamed of a dog, which turned into a glass cabinet, only to be thrown out of the window with the rest of the furniture from the seventeenth floor by a jealous husband. According to the book of dreams he consulted, this dream meant the number fifty-one. He won the lottery, decided to buy a hotel in Iquito, Peru, with his winnings and offered Raoul a job.

The terrace looked out over the riverbank. Together they built a pizza oven and watched every morning as black vultures settled on the sand by the wicker chairs. Raoul took a photo every morning of the changing patterns of these lethargic creatures.

Their guests were mostly American and German. They drank beer, which they then sweated out straightaway in the heat, complained after the first night about the mosquitoes, and left after the third.

There are seventy-four different kinds of mosquito.

XLII

In the rainy season when there were no more tourists, they closed the hotel. Raoul flew to Lima, hired a car, and drove to the Cordillera, and the ravine of Paypote.

The man at the petrol station told them stories of snowstorms that brought down a hail of stones. His brother though, he said, had been killed on a cloudless day, when the thermometer plummeted below zero.

They had only found him two years later, by the side of a mountain trail; his body was completely preserved, as if he had fallen asleep, the reins of the mule still in his hands.

XLIII

In the valley of Copiapo it smelled of carnations. Raoul spent the night on a bench in a
pub. At the bar they had been talking about a hill called Bramador – named after the
bellowing of a rutting bull.

The way up and the way down are one and the same. According to what he was told the
roar only sounded when one walked up the dune, but not down.

That turned out to be true.

XLIV

Even when he is alone, Raoul thinks back to it.
His landlady's daughter lays out his food on the oak table; the noodles are made of
coarse flour, they are still steaming and taste slightly bitter.
The oak table came from an Italian general in the Great War.
The waves break monotonously on the white sand.
Swimming is something he has never learnt.
The woman he could love would have green eyes and red hair. Between her legs it
would be paler, but thick towards her belly, like the throat of the desert fox that he leaves
his half-empty bowl for under the trees.
In the morning it is always empty.

XLV

In some dreams his hands are clenched into a fist.
The air is oppressively hot, damp, the sun not yet up.
He rarely sleeps longer than four hours.
The lights of the fishing boats are framed by the window; they flicker on the wall as the
waves rise and fall like the beam of a lighthouse.

—

XLVI

The cicadas. Behind the Peruvian hotel their dull hum emanating from the rainforest. But in the other ear an irregular, piercing whine could be heard, like a rusty lattice gate grating on its hinges in the wind, back and forth, back and forth.

The night was full of it.

These two quite distinct tones were made by one and the same animal, one no bigger than one's little finger; they remained, of all the sounds he would ever hear, the only ones which could be compared with those of the sand.

XLVII

It was in Iquito that he met Elif. That was what she called herself: Elif; it was the short form of the name she owed to her German mother.

She had nothing against her mother, she added quickly. Her father was French and she had grown up in Toulon. Meeting someone abroad, someone who comes pretty much from your own home town, creates a kind of intimacy. Sometimes it is unwelcome, and one nods slightly in passing, but ignores the other person otherwise.

That was also how it had been with Raoul and Elif.

Elif; saying the name out loud was strange.

Only weeks later did he speak to her, when it could no longer be avoided. Elif worked in the National Park as a guide, leading parties on excursions.

Often it is only the very tip of the wing that distinguishes one species of bird from another, she said, and spread out her arms.

They laughed.

That same evening they discovered they had the same birthday. That was almost too much intimacy, as in fact they couldn't have been more dissimilar. Nevertheless it still took quite a while before they recognized it themselves; love, that is.

XLVIII

Her eyes were dark, the narrow ring of the iris as dark as her pupils, which were so wide,
it seemed they could see more and further than other people.
Raoul looked at her and his looking had no end.
There was nothing unpleasant about it, not like when idle gazing gradually turns into
open staring and one has to look away.
An 'alam' is a kind of sign, Raoul explained to her, which marks the path, mostly a
small pyramid of piled-up stones, often simply a broken water jug or a stick in the sand.
Once, on our way to Korizo, we passed an abandoned oilfield. There were containers
standing about, drilling gear, and there was also a pump room with a metal door; a pipe
protruded from the concrete floor inside.
If a bit of gravel is thrown down inside, and one begins counting, one hears nothing,
nothing at all, until forty-eight. When it hits the water, it is like rock being fissured, a
loud hiss, surging up in waves and only gradually fading.

XLIX

Elif had shown him the birds. She could see them with the naked eye, while he, even with binoculars, mostly scanned the branches in vain. Through the lenses, the trees were unrecognizable, as if the magnification distorted everything. She set up a tripod for him, adjusted it, and suddenly splashes of red and blue leapt from the foliage, as if they were totally unreal, as if one was looking into a kaleidoscope.

She called the sand-bird by pressing her lips on her open palm and breathing in wetly and loudly, with a smack, a kiss. It answered the call each time, but always from a different place; for an hour they followed carefully, until at last Elif spotted it sitting on a cocoa tree, like a shrivelled leaf, in all the shades of ochre, the white line under its throat like a stalk.

L

He won't ever speak about private things, of that Raoul is sure.

What was her star sign? asks Török's wife.

Raoul has drunk too much; that'd be the only reason to respond at all to a question like that, he says contemptuously.

They were all Scorpio.

Török's wife almost bursts out laughing; but she manages to keep a straight face.

He never calls her by her first name. That is not a sign of disrespect, no. In truth he does it only because he envies Török.

Sometimes he seems slightly lost, in spite of his sullen moods, don't you think? says Török's wife to her husband, as he comes into the kitchen carrying the dishes.

In the dusk outside the window, the tree looks as if it was only rooted in the earth so as not to drift out into the dark.

LI

At first he said nothing, but then he repeated it over and over again, when they were sitting opposite each other eating, when he was walking along next to her, or she suddenly turned her profile towards the light: she was the most beautiful woman he had ever seen. And a smile played across his face as he said it, which almost made him appear handsome to her.

He courted her, would bring her little presents, which he made with his own hands; it was as if he had learned everything from the other two women, only to see her happy now.

Ugly men often cling to unshakeable convictions such as this.

LII

They had agreed on the night that they would sleep together for the first time. Raoul
went into the forest and cut as many orchids as he could; the chef helped him. He spread
the ones that had not been crushed in the rucksack out over the bed (that only seems
exaggerated here; there are types of orchids that are all root).
Still wearing a shirt she slipped under the mosquito net.
Raoul whispered everything she could become for him into her navel. Her breasts,
he said, were like the warm quivering breasts of sparrows. That was a poetic sentence, the
only one that would occur to him, ever.
It did not overcome her shyness, though.
That had nothing to do with the bed; in bed she was as close to him as could be. There
she would whisper into his ear how long it would be before the moment came; the
moment, she said.
And yet, it was as if he could never really peel away a layer and bring her out of herself.
He was self-conscious about his clumsy, awkward fingers that never seemed to know
what to do with her soft skin. He tried hard, searched for resistance and found it between
her legs.
Not so quickly, said Elif, and he jerked back, only to lose himself again.

LIII

Let there be no doubt. She was beautiful, extraordinarily beautiful. Even Francesca had said that, when she visited them with her latest fiancé.

Elif had narrow shoulders, curls of hair falling right down her back. In Egypt people took her for Arab, he tells Török's wife, expecting some kind of complicity in exchange, in Israel for Jewish, and in France for French.

She was in every way the opposite of Arlette.

And once again he had been mistaken about the bodies of women, noticing only much later how Elif did everything she could to hide her large bottom by swinging her hips or slinging a big towel round them.

A solid rump, she said, full of contempt, without really expecting him to contradict.

An hourglass, he replied nevertheless.

At night the light from a lamp in front of the hotel would fall through the open panel in the door, so that it seemed to be always just before daybreak. Sometimes it was stormy; then the river rolled against the bank so that the bed began to sway gently.

He asked her again and again to just stay in that light. He loved nothing more than seeing her standing there naked like that.

As to why that was, he had no idea, just as he was in the dark about other things: Elif had recognized that instinctively.

But that was not the reason.

Her back, the faint sheen that seemed to come from her skin, all this was a kind of promise.

So he looked at her secretly, as soon as she felt herself unobserved. But Elif saw through that straight away too. She could not bear it, locked the bathroom door, avoiding anything that reflected her at all.

It was as if nothing could reconcile her to her body. Not even the few words that Raoul was capable of saying. The words were never the right ones. And his hands did not know how to make up for all that was missing.

LIV

Only sometimes, and only when she was in bed, she would sit with her back to him, holding onto his legs.

Her shoulder blade, her collarbone.

His cock and the pink seam of her legs. The brown of the anus and the white of the skin.

There was no lust and nothing to touch with their fingers. Something hard.

Only each of them opening for the other, so that they were completed by the other: it is hard to find a word for what Raoul was thinking.

And always too brief. Too far away.

LV

Everything is always contained in its origin. Raoul had made the mistake of telling Elif about Arlette and Francesca. He explained it as one might explain a riddle, hoping that someone else would provide
the solution.

'For a dog it has the same side (5 letters)' was the clue for five across in the crossword puzzle of the newspaper that he and the chef had subscribed to, and which always turned up two weeks late. Neither of them had enough English to work it out. Elif though simply understood Raoul's stories as awkward paraphrases of the expectations he seemed to confront her with. Nothing he said, nor the nights they spent together, could change that.

Only the chef knew what to make of it all. Beautiful women, he explained, giving Raoul a friendly punch in the stomach, are always insecure, God only knows why; men, however, if they find themselves in the presence of a beautiful woman, become crude. The reason is simple: they think they will never have them and that makes them coarse.

As far as crude remarks went, there was no shortage for Elif to bear. That she hardly ever took them as compliments, which they might have been intended to be, is understandable. But that did nothing to alter the fact that she was instructed to be a bit friendlier towards the tourists, otherwise she would find herself spending a good deal more time with her typewriter.

The official in charge of the National Park was a man too.

Raoul returned with her to France.

That was the only reason.

LVI

El Punto del Diablo in South America, Bir el Abbes in Algeria. The Mountain of the Bell in Mexico. Mountains of dunes, thousands of metres above the Sea of China, in the Namib desert, the Kalahari; a droning, thundering, and rumbling echoing back. Beaches in Vietnam, Thailand, and the Aleutians, where people imagine they hear animal calls in the rattling of the sand.

To others the world becomes whole through other places, other things. Maybe there is an idea of innocence behind it; or at least the desire for one.

If it remains unfulfilled and the loneliness lasts too long, then one is ready to confess anything to anyone. To Török's wife, he says one thing, to both of them together something else, and this despite the fact that to him even the very first words have already betrayed too much.

An admission of weakness.

If one gives in to it, one also wants to see the depth and extent of it. It is like when the sand gives way underfoot. Perhaps a distinct voice will make itself heard above the rushing, something Raoul has failed to hear up until now: an omen, if one wants to call it that.

Raoul tells Török about the orchids; he feels bad about it afterwards. Török reacts to these unwanted intimacies like most of us do, by feeling slightly disconcerted and trying hard to appear interested.

Commonplaces.

To see the world in a grain of sand in the palm of one's hand, the world in an orchid; but you don't like books, says Török, and it seems unintentionally mocking.

It is like with proverbs, responds Raoul. They are all true and therefore contradict one another.

LVII

Tell me a story, Elif had said. And make it come true.

LVIII

There was once a Public Writer in Dun Huang who had a daughter called Crescent Moon. He idolized her, and saw in her every gesture the gestures of his wife, who had died in childbirth. Each year on the anniversary he would hold a great feast that he spent months beforehand preparing. So it was that mourning and joy coincided and became one and the same.

Among his friends was a general, who had grown tired of his troops and battle. Together they would spend their evenings constructing rockets for the tiny painstakingly fashioned wooden casings that they filled with glitter and coloured powder. The fireworks set the stars alight in a blaze of colour; that was the highpoint of the celebrations every year.

It was the day of her thirteenth birthday when a great wind blew up and fanned the sparks on the tent where the feast was being celebrated. A young musician called Sha-shan-ze saw that flames were already licking about her hair.

He took her head in his arms, pressed her to his breast to smother the fire, but caught light himself. Henceforth he would see before him the astonished look of her eyes, the narrow eyelids like water-lily petals, her face as bright as a stone under a flowing brook.

For ten years he did not set eyes on her. Then, one night in the Mogao Caves where he was playing the lute for the nocturnal festival of the Thousand Buddhas, he saw her again. Crescent Moon recognized Sha-shan-ze at once by the burn mark on his cheek and fell in love with him.

Her father, however, refused to give them his blessing because the musician was penniless.

I understand you, said the Public Writer to Crescent Moon. Without music the heavens would be empty and silent as the grave; music allows us to hear the turning of the earth, like when a top is spinning on a table-top, and the wood starts to sing faintly as it spins; one feels it in one's fingertips.

But, the Public Writer said to Crescent Moon, a musician presses his ear to this emptiness to hear the note that lies beyond the silence. Yet he will never manage to capture that note in his strings for a second time; his fingertips search again and again for a new note; the silence of the heavens permits no repetition.

Even a spinning top, once released from its string . . .

A woman nevertheless . . .

The Public Writer did not pursue either of the parables to its conclusion, which shows that he was a wise man indeed. But Crescent Moon guessed what it was he wanted to tell her. She thought of the firework, the constellations that it sketches for a moment across the night sky, that they seem more beautiful even than a lover.

And what of the General? Crescent Moon asked her father. He had never addressed a single word to her in all the years she had known him. The rockets, however, that he filled with powder came, with each passing year, to resemble more closely the shape of a bird as they burned away, a bird with bright blue tail-feathers and wings that at last reached out to fill the night sky. And his gaze, which rested on her as she brought the tea for him and her father, it became more and more taciturn.

It was on her birthday that he let off the most beautiful firework he had ever made, and they were wed.

But the fire in Sha-shan-ze was still smouldering like the embers in a covered wooden bowl that one takes for a long journey. Sometimes it kept him warm in the mountains bordering the Sinjiang province when he took his lute at night to play in the snow. His fingers never became numb, but soon he began to cough and he faded away so that he had to be taken to a monastery. On his deathbed at last he asked to be buried half way along the path to the cave of the Thousand Buddhas.

The Crescent Moon visited his grave on top of which a dune slowly grew, and each time she shed a tear. When the wind rose, she heard the sand singing; it sounded like a string was being tuned to the wind.

Then years of storms came, years of harvest, years of drought, and again years of sun and storms. The General was buried with full honours, and there was nothing she missed anymore, for missing is something bodily.

But as the Crescent Moon set behind the mountain of the Thousand Buddhas forever, the earth all around the dune of Ming Sha Shan broke open and the water gushed forth. That is how it came to pass that the two of them were united for all eternity and the crescent of a lake came to lie at the foot of a dune.

LIX

All the places and the list of their names. It is difficult to say exactly what his travels meant to Raoul. He himself scarcely thought about them at all; after the trip from Grosseto to Japan, they had become almost second nature to him. No: that is only half true, just as every voyage is only itself a half.

Every journey, he could feel it, wore something out. For each one he cast something off, like one might remove a coat, a pullover, a shirt. It took a layer, a thickness of skin. Underneath in some places a blankness would appear, something brittle, that no longer held together. As if there was nothing whole anymore. As if the words were getting fewer and fewer, as if it became more and more difficult to speak.

In the desert, one dresses warmly and in dark clothes; one drinks tea.

Francesca, Arlette, Elif, Francesca.

With each name Raoul associates a home, without finding it. And yet it is the only thing he can get close to.

Elif, Francesca, Arlette; Elif.

With each one he becomes more silent, withdrawing further into himself. All the distance he can feel coming from him. With each time the longing grows, with each time he moves further away from something.

The body is only one of those things.

LX

A dried-up riverbed, or the arms of a delta, drought; a bush, some pebble or other, even a termite mound, sometimes: it's all the wind needs.

In the wind cornices line up and grow up into dunes; they form chains and banks, they take on the shape of an egg, a heart, or a star.

The suspended load of the wind; it blows each grain of sand from windward, hardly higher than a foot or two off the ground, until they are pressed together on the crest, only to slip down the steep face in its lee; it is just the same as with waves.

The wind drives them before it.

Some get stuck and become as round as whalebacks. Others collide, roll over, and leave a nascent dune behind them; these grotesque imitations of life might easily disturb someone with too much imagination.

A flat drift of sand that accumulates, let's say, behind a bush, is called *nebka*. The thin blades of the seif lie in the direction of the wind; the expression is Arabic for sword. The long sickles of parabolic dunes on the other hand face into the wind, they trail their flanks behind them, still clinging to any trace of moisture, limping on.

If the wind dries them out they turn within a matter of days and become barchans, which roam with the wind, a few steps before it, their arms pointing downwind.

Draa is the name of the labyrinth built up by lines and grids of dunes; in the ripples of sand on their curved backs everything repeats itself, on the most minute scale.

If the wind meets a cliff, the sand gets heaped up against it, upwind; the ensuing turbulence opens up a corridor.

Oases and paths can often be found inside.

Such dunes are called echo-dunes.

LXI

Sand seas are eroded mountains and deposits of rivers. Sometimes they consist
almost entirely of evaporated seawater; the gypsum is blinding.
Feldspar and quartz.
Gravel or grit, siliceous or ferruginous. Sands of lead or lime; but where the sand of
the great deserts comes from, no one knows for sure; it takes a million years to
migrate a hundred kilometres downstream.
The wind is indiscriminate, however; it is the water that sieves the sand.
In the South Seas the sand consists mainly of volcanic particles. The white beaches of
the atolls, however, are made up of the microscopic creatures of the reef, brightly
coloured corals worn away by the waves, whorl-shaped snail-shells, single-celled
foraminifers, fragments of mussels, the star-shaped needles of sea-sponges, the lime
of minuscule pieces of green algae growing in submarine pastures of grass.

LXII

There is one subject which Raoul and Török would like to discuss in greater
depth, but if they don't, it's because there is nothing that can be said about it for
certain. Guesswork exhausts itself quickly.

You remember no doubt the scene in *Lawrence of Arabia* where Peter O'Toole
returns as a hero, bringing with him the Arab who had fallen from his camel in his
sleep?

But that's not the one.

It is the one a few scenes later, where he stands by helplessly, as his servant Daud is
swallowed by quicksand.

The question is whether such a thing really exists.

Quicksand, *Treibsand, sables mouvants*; these are the names of the loose, wet sand
which is found along the mudflats of many coastlines; it is the water that prevents it
from becoming firm.

But in the desert?

LXIII

All the places and their times. They are repeated, without one becoming conscious of their recurrence. At least three points are needed to construct a circle; that is how one finds its centre.
But what if, as in reality, they lie in a straight line?
What use is spherical geometry then?
The shearing forces in dunes, the characteristics of different types of sand will still not be calculable.

LXIV

Török's wife has a half-sister whose brother did his military service at an outpost on
the Egyptian border where the commanding officer had in turn been told by a local
guide that there was quicksand in the Great Sand Sea.

The camels, so the story went, had smelled the spot already from afar, although it
was scarcely distinguishable from its surroundings, even to the sharp eyes of the
driver. They then came to a halt, stubbornly refusing to move onto the field of sand,
where, when struck by a stick, shallow waves would ebb back and forth,

as if from one shore to another.

Faults, ice ages, and oceans drying up.

Periods and epochs.

Precambrian, Archaean, the Holocene. The sand ground down to a fine dust, peeled
away, split, and of untold depths.

Perhaps, suggests Török, it is clay that has been deposited in the basin; the fine silt
on the bed of what once was a lake. But then the heat and the rain would have baked it
into a solid crust, the wind hardened it into sediment.

LXV

And then? asks Török. His wife comes back from the kitchen carrying halva. Raoul
keeps talking; he is talking more and more for her alone.
Elif finally found a job in Monaco, at the Institute for Marine Biology; I found one
with a balloon pilot in Avignon. I would follow in a pickup to retrieve the balloon
each time and bring it back.
The wind turns in all directions.
Once we had a couple of rich gay Americans in the basket, who wanted to
plight their troth up there; it took me days to find the diamond ring that they threw out
of the basket.
On another occasion Jacques, that was his name, touched down in the inner courtyard
of a farmhouse belonging to an Egyptian. No one was there, not even a caretaker or
gardener, nobody, and on the gate was a notice saying that the house was booby-
trapped.
Jacques?
Another short-term companion, I'd reckon.
He developed, Raoul continues, a special technique of stopping the balloon in free
fall. Once he used it to land on the roof of a house. The silk of the balloon fell down
across the facade, right over the balcony, and covered the window. The old woman, who
suddenly found herself sitting in the dark, cried out because she thought the end of the
world had come.
Sometimes Elif came to visit me at the weekends, and during the week I would travel
to Monaco. At her place I was always only ever a guest. When I had to leave, she
wished me back; but when I was there, I could not be gone soon enough for her.
One has to love twice as much so as to be left with at least half.
In all this the wind tends to be forgotten.

LXVI

When Raoul looks out from his window over the sea, the sun sets. To the north, somewhere, there is Italy and Grosseto.

In the east the earth's shadow is rising. The water is grey and blue; it is deceptive, sometimes appearing a silvery white. When it is hazy it becomes almost violet. Where the wind drops there are long bright streaks in the water revealing the currents.

All this has no importance, but it helps.

At least it is somehow soothing.

The flashing lights of the planes are quite easily distinguishable from the stars.

The beach is filthy. It adjoins a piece of land which is surrounded by a wall kilometres long, a firing range for the military. They do target practice there, and the wind drags trails of dust and the detonations from each impact right to the house.

LXVII

Elif is far away. Sometimes Raoul calls her; she immediately hangs up. There is
nothing to be done; nothing to wait for. He has tried it, so he thinks, from all 360
degrees of the compass.
Where north is, the devil only knows.
In the east, they were together. It was a long journey, one that he had wanted to make;
perhaps Elif too, who knows.

LXVIII

They came from Paris via Hong Kong and Shanghai and arrived in north-west China.
A runway in the middle of a cornfield. A herd of pigs in the first light. The Hoang-Ho,
yellow with silt, the banks hollowed out: Lanzhou.

Yet it is not by listing the names of places that the earth becomes round. It just
unfurls before one like a rolled map that never seems to come to an end; that is how it
is with every story.

The confusion of signs, names, faces; language.

Entering the country. Checkpoints, misunderstandings, and waiting, hunched on a low
bench with one's arms wrapped round one's knees. Elif burst into tears and then fell
asleep on Raoul's shoulder.

At midnight the translator arrived, the representative from the Ministry, the employee
from the travel company, the guide, and the driver. They did not get to bed until the
early hours; but the programme began as had been agreed at 7 a.m.

Maybe I never loved her again as much as I did in those helpless, all too brief
exhausted hours of sleep.

That is the sort of thing one claims in retrospect, claims Török.

LXIX

From Lanzhou the journey continued north towards the desert. The four of them sat in the cab of an old Russian lorry: the guide, the driver and the two of them. After a while their cheeks were aching from smiling as they listened.

The landscapes passed by: carts, horses, and people.

At each dip in the road the translator, sitting in the back with the payload, was jolted up in the air. At every stop, and there were lots of them, as every fifty kilometres the leaky radiator needed to be filled up, he would translate what the driver had said as he chattered on without pause, constantly pointing to right and left.

Once, long ago, an old hermit had lived in the desert who believed himself to be in a state of the most pure virtue, so one of the stories went; he had asked God what was still lacking in him, and had asked him to grant it.

On hearing this, God sent him to the nearest village, to the Village Elder, whom he had told in a dream what he should do, were the hermit really to appear before him. The man came and he knocked at his door. They embraced, sat down, and then the hermit asked the old man what he should do in order to know bliss.

Will you do whatever I tell you? the Village Elder asked him. And the hermit replied: Yes.

Then take this staff and go and tend these sows.

The people who knew the hermit and now saw him with his herd of pigs thought that his mind had become confused; he is possessed, they said, by the devil, who now even conceals himself in sows. And the rumour did the rounds.

When the translator reached this point, the driver guffawed, his toothless mouth open wide.

LXX

From Lanzhou they continued to Wuwei and from there to Jinchang, and thence to Yabrai Yanchang. The driver remained silent, as the mountains became highland, the highlands descended, gave way to rocky plains and the rocky plains became a valley, where they set up camp.

At the neck of the gorge, the stream was lined with amber trees (*Liquidambar orientalis*), their leaves as serrated and grey as the bark.

If one clapped one's hands they fell. They fell, only to be lifted up off the ground in a swarm, shining red, with black dots and white stripes.

The butterflies (*Callimorpha quadripunctaria*) came to this valley to find moisture in the cool shade, and to mate. After the long flight, however, most of them were exhausted and died.

The names in brackets had been added by the translator, who was a trained biologist, had obtained permission to have a second child, and could never quite look them in the eye.

Elif was happy. She strolled under the trees that gave off a strong scent and collected leaves. Raoul slept on the back of the lorry, so she could have the tent to herself.

In the fierce blaze the trees were bare, the sparks and wings one; the fire attracting them.

LXXI

Raoul Louper got up to walk down to the water. He lost his way, wandered for three days in the darkness, and at last, at the end of his strength, fell to the ground ready to die. A small boy appeared before him with bread and a pitcher of water in his hands: Stand up and eat, he said.

Raoul got up and prayed; he thought a devil had appeared to him.

And the child said: It is good.

And he prayed again, and a second and a third time.

And the child said: It is good.

Raoul was shaken awake by the driver; they loaded up the vehicle.

LXXII

From Yabrai Yanchang to the north, always to the north. Then they left the lorry
behind in Bojitoreganor and continued on camels.

Many things are contained within others, and not only in names; in the north there is
also a south and a west. The Badain Jaran desert is indeed to be found within the
Gobi desert. But it too contains within it the Takla Makan. And within that again,
somewhere there, even if not precisely there and now, lies the untouched centre of the
earth, the Desert of Lop.

In the beginning everything was simply a plain. The rain came from the heavens and
it rose and rose, never quite reaching this centre. And it lasted, lasted as long as it
takes a tortoise to drink the sea dry, or an ant to walk round the globe.

Only then did the mountains descend from the firmament, and lined up all around.
From them the wind detached itself and brought the sands; it piled them up into peaks
and cliffs, slopes, ramparts, and walls. Between them the lakes were left behind, many
thousands of feet above sea level, as high as the flood had risen; a great blue, the
reeds and all the birds, soaring above them.

Possibly only in one's imagination.

Light falling vertically, so that there is neither distance nor nearness, only direction.

LXXIII

The dunes had the silhouettes of pyramids, larger ones standing out against the smaller ones. It takes days to get that far.

The route to reach them is the path of the ant lions.

Those are the larvae of the virgin ants (Myrmeleontidae, family of lacewinged insects), Elif was told.

They dig funnel-shaped pits in the sandy ground and catch the insects that happen to slide to the bottom.

LXXIV

To get further north than the summit is impossible. Or, for that matter, any other direction.

The colours changed imperceptibly with each step that took them higher up. Then the ridge fell away sharply and the view opened out across this sand sea, its ground swell, the dunes.

The guide sat down on the slope, pushed himself down with his feet, ran his hand, then his arm through the sand.

The rushing became muffled, like lumps of stone being battered against each other by the surf and rolling down into the hollow.

As soon as evening fell, the sound set in along with the wind and echoed all around. It carried far, long-drawn-out cries like the moaning of whales underwater, under tons of water.

LXXV

The sand on the coast and in the desert create two quite distinct sounds. One is high-pitched (500–2,500 Hz); it lasts scarcely a second, buzzing like a thread of wax stretched between one's teeth and one's hand. In the desert it is most easily heard when the sun is at its zenith; on a shore, just after the top layer of sand has been dried out.

The other sound is much deeper (50–250 Hz); it comes in waves, says the translator, and the flanks of the dune gave way again and slipped further down so that one could feel it rippling through one's body, on and on.

It's particularly impressive after a sandstorm; that was the first sentence to be heard from their guide.

The driver was much less interested in all this; his attention was fixed on something entirely different. Elif was bounding down as fast as she could, with long strides, singing at the top of her voice, in high spirits, almost happy.

And the camels stretching their necks in time with it.

LXXVI

On the very top of the dune, exactly on the line of the crest, lay a chalk-white stone, the size of a clenched fist. How it could have got there, no one can say.

Maybe this stone had been the one obstacle in the path of the wind that had led the chain of dunes to form this erg; perhaps the sand had lifted it higher and higher, always in this precarious balance, never allowing it to tip over.

Elif picked it up; she gave it to Raoul that evening at the camp. It is this stone he has put in a window alcove together with the greegree and the pine cone.

LXXVII

Elif. Francesca. Arlette. In each case, there is just a comma between the three names.

Sometimes Raoul sits in front of the house, the whitewashed wall is warm, and he thinks of all three at the same time. No, he remembers and often confuses them, calls one of them by the name of one of the others.

Nothing lies in the past, hardly anything that still matters now.

Sometimes a freighter is visible; the nearest port is Alexandria.

It is difficult to keep everything apart.

Raoul had begun to tell the story to Török; now he is telling it, as has already been said, to his wife.

For himself he finds things other than words.

LXXVIII

That evening in the Badain Jaran desert had been perfectly silent, until it suddenly began to drone, and Elif had to shout to make herself understood at all.
The rushing of a second dune started up, crackling like a great fire, the booming of a third one swelled and then set in deeper than the others but in tune with the first, so that gradually a rhythm became discernible.
This strange chorus lasted for a long, long time; then silence returned and the ground stopped trembling once more.

LXXIX

The search for your dunes, Raoul had finally understood.

It is like the sand-bird, Elif explained to him, as they were sitting by the campfire, staring at it, silent.

One covers the embers with ashes, so that they can be rekindled the next morning. In winter one digs a flat trough, shovels them into it, covering them with sand to keep warm at night.

They lay side by side; but what mattered was how near she slept to him.

The sleeping bags smelled of smoke.

LXXX

A few years ago, I discovered a dune that no one had heard of. It was on the border with Chad, not far from the spot where the wreckage of Arafat's shot-down plane still lies.

We had pitched the tents in a hollow and had already eaten; I only clambered up to the top because I wanted to have a pee under the stars.

Coming down a dune, one begins to run involuntarily. However, I stopped and stood still, as I thought I could hear some kind of vehicle approaching, a military patrol perhaps. But up on the crest everything was quiet again; and headlights would have been visible from some distance.

Back at the camp, the others would not believe me at first. But I was not even half-way back down when the noise started up again like a motor running.

At last I realized that it was coming from my footsteps and the sand I dislodged with each step, but only on this part of the slope, and not to the right or left of it.

LXXXI

This is the last time there will be any discussion of the creation of dunes. But for that it is necessary to understand how sand is transported by the wind.

If it reaches a critical speed above loose ground (usually about 20 km/h), the grains begin to move by fits and starts; they jump.

Caught in their parabolic trajectories, the grains of sand begin to rotate, knocking together and emitting sparks. The stronger the wind, the higher they will be carried, until they begin to irritate the eye; caught in one's lashes, they rub under the lids, get enflamed, burn.

Blown against any surface in the path of the wind, they will pile up until a wind shadow arises: a dune is nothing else.

Often they lie for kilometres on end in the lee of table mountains; the testimony to an eroded range.

Only beyond a certain angle (between 32° and 34°) does the sand begin to slide down in cascades.

The bedrock underneath then becomes a kind of resonant body, comparable to the soundbox of an instrument.

Tongues of flame, in midair.

LXXXII

'Sam' might derive from the word for fire, 'andar' from 'inside'. Salamander though is not an animal, but rather a substance found in the earth; it is not in any animal's nature to live in fire, as every living creature is made up of all four elements in different proportions.

Down from the dune that was marked with two red flags, the camels returned by following their own tracks; then they drove west, always further west.

The guide, it just occurs to me now, was called Yuan.

But it was the driver who told us about salamander stone being dug out of seams in the mountainside. Pounded and crushed, the substance split into threads like wool spread out in the sun.

The entrances to the mineshafts were visible on the flanks, black as coal. Once dried, the asbestos is ground in a kind of copper mortar and all the earth washed out. Then the fibres are spun into a cloth turning white in the fire.

It was difficult, if not totally impossible, to decipher the truth from the intonation of the translator, or to guess it from his gestures. His temples were already bald, instead the hair on the back of his head stood up in tufts.

LXXXIII

Raoul saw her as they drove past. She was standing at the edge of the road, with a stick in her hand, a dog restless at her side. She stood without moving, her face without expression. Her eyes green, like grass when the wind blows through it and turns the stalks white. The sleeves of her dress red, as if dipped in red ochre; dyed.

LXXXIV

It is no longer me telling this story. It has long since grown beyond the evenings in Cairo, the table with its chessboard pattern of tiles.

Török is standing on the balcony.

His wife is leaning on the doorframe. Raoul sits in his chair in the shadow of the lamp.

There is a moment in the telling of any story when things get so close that the contours start to dissolve; then it's better to be silent.

LXXXV

The province of Kamul lies between two deserts; its oases are known for their melons and grapes, its people for taking life easy, enjoying a party, singing and dancing.
And it is true that the hospitality there also extends to their women; the men leave their house for the duration of the stranger's visit and only return once he has decided to leave.
Even the Great Khan was not able to forbid this custom, says Raoul, and avoids looking Török straight in the eye.

LXXXVI

In the province of Tangut we stumbled upon a procession that had stopped in
front of a wooden house covered with brightly coloured silk cloths. There they set
down the bier with the dead body, and placed wine and bread in flasks and baskets
before it. We all joined in the meal, Elif and Raoul too.

Flutes and drums.

Towards evening the cortege made its way to a place where tinder had been gathered
and piled up. Figures had been cut out of paper and cardboard; people, painted horses
and camels, which were laid by the side of the corpse. The fire kept going out until
the guide fetched a can of petrol from the lorry.

The sheets of paper, which had been coated with tin on one side, turn to silver in the
flames; the smoke sends it up to the souls in their dark heavens. Many families also
fold the paper into hollow ingots; that takes a good deal of work and some skill, but
increases the value of the treasure immeasurably.

LXXXVII

Eighty-seven miles beyond the settlement, we drove through a camp, where men were looking for gold illegally. They attacked the lorry with metal bars, pipes, and axes and only retreated when the driver fired his rifle into the air. People seldom drive along that piste.

The towns of Wuwei, Yumen, and Anshi.

There would be stories to tell, of individual encounters, the broken suspension that had to be bound together with moistened threads of hemp, gearboxes which would no longer work, tyres patched up somehow or other.

But all these are things that anyway remain in one's memory, no matter what happens.

LXXXVIII

And Elif? She simply could no longer bear the silence, the distance; the dependency on one another that they brought with them.

Reg, deserts of gravel. Angular ventifacts, facets of red, yellow, orange, almost green.

The landscape, as it became hard, and the cold; one's skin getting chafed.

It was a way of being alone with one another that nothing would assuage.

Sediment of a dried-out lake, eroded by the wind into bizarre needles and towers. The presentiment of a world resting only upon time itself.

A violence bursting forth, making each movement abrupt.

Raoul brought her tea. Held her in his arms, covered her head with them, stroking her.

Everything inside her struggled against it. With Yuan, the guide, she felt safe, for the most part; that's not much, scarcely enough.

LXXXIX

Nothing can compare to a moonless night there; the constellations like flagstones in such clear relief against the sky that they cast shadows, the Milky Way, where they join together again above the light. And all of it like an idea, not of nearness, but of clearness.

In the camp, however, the tents were pitched closer each evening, as if by doing that a human presence could be asserted.

Each breath was audible. They did not sleep with each other, also because they were too tired. Sleeping with somebody was the only way Elif knew of giving herself up into someone else's hands.

So they grew further apart with each day; and with their intimacy, their trust vanished also.

XC

In the afternoon the temperature fell twenty degrees within one hour. For two days we
stayed in the tents which we had lashed down on to the lorries.

The air became thick, the sun blackened beyond the walls. For a while that kept the
wind at bay, but then it found a way, bursting through, flinging up volumes of sand,
mixed with gravel and stone. The faster it got dark, the more intensely the wind
burned; burning like a furnace, in which quartz melts, becoming glass.

On the Egyptian coast now the sand will be spattering against the windowpane
of Raoul's room; from the south the khamsin is blowing, the wind that earned its name
because it lasts for fifty days.

It is the only thing that might help against remembering.

XCI

Dun Huang got its name from the fire beacon of the watchtower which was once used to warn against invaders from the west.

Ten-storey buildings in the centre, farmsteads built of mud bricks on the outer fringes, fields, vines, fruit trees, and palms.

A street with garage yards, another with tailors' shops, a third of oil drums filled with steaming noodles; the stalls on the market under electric lights.

Under the rule of the Tibetans or the Tanguts or the Mongols, the oasis was called Shachow, 'City of Sands'; it was destroyed and rebuilt, but the old Chinese name stuck.

Women, their wares spread out on a headscarf, music at full volume from ghetto-blasters, a popcorn seller, horse-drawn taxis, shooting booths, women who read palms.

In the hotel the bare concrete floor; water had to be fetched in buckets from the bar, but there was a bed. And all that had remained unspoken between her and him, and all that of which I know nothing.

XCII

The caves of the Thousand Buddhas lie fifteen kilometres south of Dun Huang. Travellers, wandering monks and scholars, their votive offerings there and in the monasteries and abbeys nearby. Hsung-tsang, the 'Master of the Law', brought back ninety-two holy Buddhist texts from his pilgrimages in India, which had lasted many years, and wanted to translate them into Chinese.

The frescoes depict scenes from the Buddha's youth, images of paradise, demons and monsters, sandstorms and mountain peaks under threatening cloud. Little Buddha figures have been drawn in charcoal on the ceilings and walls; I do not know if anybody has ever taken the trouble to count them.

The river has cut through the rock face; just as many countless visitors have worn steps into the rock, which are treacherously slippery.

In one of the caves there is a chamber which has been sealed for centuries, the translator explained. It was a Hungarian who broke it open, bribed the monks, and finally deposited twenty-four chests full of rolls of parchment in the British Museum.

The driver had stayed in the lorry. Elif stood by the poplar trees (*Populus diversifolia*), which lined the road and formed an arch of dense foliage.

XCIII

Dwarf poplars have taken root all round the lake of the Crescent Moon, a few kilometres
from Dun Huang in the dunes; in another fifty years they will probably have reached
the oasis.

With the constantly changing wind the lines of the ridges change too; flags of sand
billow in the air from the summit. During the day the hollows and slopes remain in
the shade; but the crests shimmer like ice, the colour of the wind.

The quartz particles, turquoise blue and royal blue, lapis lazuli, emerald green,
carnelian, vermilion and scarlet, heliotrope and amber, grey and white, spread
out on a map-sheet, and the sand becoming iridescent, the entire cataract of light.

The erg stretches from west to east, parallel to the mountains of Kuruk Tagh;
between them lies the desert of Lop.

XCIV

So many people and names, just for this one simple story. The driver was called Song, the translator Chiang-ssuh-yeh.

We all climbed up the dune, ran alone or together down its face, each time in a different place, at least ankle-deep without ever falling over ourselves.

Once I clasped Elif's hands as we went down.

The driver had stayed in the car. The sand no longer sings, he said, since the chimneys of Dun Huang started belching out so much coal dust.

XCV

The desert of Lop Nor stretches between the north-east and the east; the few wells there are brackish and bitter.

In the middle there is a perfectly flat plain of fine gravel, where the earth becomes a flat disc again and the horizon closes upon itself in a circle until, in the very middle of this, the high backs of three ochre-coloured dunes loom up, one after the other, three of them.

The traveller who comes to this nameless region will perhaps find the tracks of a mantis traced in the sand, wingless and as long as a finger. As for the insect itself, with its sand-coloured camouflage, it is only ever seen when it leaps up, startled by someone's footsteps; it is commonly known as the praying mantis (genus of *Eremiaphila*).

It lives on insects that the wind sometimes carries across hundreds of kilometres to the three dunes; the water it needs to survive is also taken from its prey.

They say that it takes a year to ride from one end to the other, but a month at the very least.

CXVI

On the edge of the desert of Lop lies the dried-up lake of Lop Nor and the long-abandoned town of Lew Sha.

On the way we met a shepherd who claimed to be over a hundred years old; his son was the only one who still understood his language. The landscape was no longer recognizable, he said; once there were villages in the reeds, fish, otters, and ducks on the lake. The earth is full of saltpetre, the translator added.

In the north there is a prohibited military site where they detonate atomic warheads. In the vicinity of Lew Sha the fragments of an exploded titanium rocket lie scattered on the ground; they glint in the dark.

Of the town itself only wood and clay remains and an occasional door post. Dead trees hacked back to stumps by nomads line the riverbed. Beyond that, extending to the very horizon, is the basin of what was once the lake, wave after wave under a layer of shor, warped salt crusts over the mud.

Only with the greatest difficulty did we manage to get the lorry back on track; it sank within minutes down to its axles and deeper.

There was nothing we could do but turn round.

XCVII

Of the desert of Lop it is said: if travellers ride through the night and one of them falls behind or asleep in the saddle, and then tries to catch up with the caravan, he will hear spirits speaking, and think them his companions. Sometimes they will call him by his name and lead him astray; in this way a great many have died.

Sometimes wandering travellers will hear something like hoof-beats and the clamour of voices from a cavalcade of riders, far from the right path and they will follow in their wake; but at daybreak they realize it was all a delusion and their situation becomes perilous.

But in daylight the demons can also be heard, the rattling of weapons, sometimes even different types of musical instrument; but mostly the beating of drums. One can see them too, their fluttering banners and the glance of their swords, as one is pursued by the whispered words: Do not be afeard! Do not be afeard!

For this reason travellers crossing the desert of Lop are careful not to lose sight of each other; the animals have little bells tied round their neck, so that the caravan does not get separated. And it has become a custom, even before striking camp, to mark the direction in which the caravan will head off the next morning with a sign. That's why I have laid out white stones in the sand for Elif in the shape of an arrow.

I know there has hardly been any mention of me. But it is me that is listening now to Elif talking, Elif, who is sitting on a chair, her eyes huge and shining in the dusk. Raoul once . . . she says; but I am not Raoul.

XCVIII

The guide had warned us about spirits hidden in the earth and the air. Some are good, he said, some bad, and they are to be found haunting the wastelands. As if that is the only place where people imagine their fear and the lack of any divine providence, says Raoul; for him it is a difficult sentence.

In Egypt it was the duty of Osiris in his human incarnation to guard the narrow strip of fertile ground along the Nile, isn't that right? Török's wife asks with a glance at her husband.

The night has become noisy. She leaves the open door of the balcony and sits down beside Raoul; their elbows are touching.

He found an enemy in Seth, and in her mouth the words took on an unexpectedly scornful tone, the ruler of the desert, its sun and its storms; he was always pictured with a crooked snout, panting, and with square ears sticking up.

Török has turned round; now it is him who goes out onto the balcony. He turns his back on them defiantly, but it seems as if he is determined to know nothing, to understand nothing. In any case they hear him murmuring, that it is written in the itinerarium of Apollonius of Tyana that he had seen such a ghoul on a dune in the moonlight; and he too had a stiff prick turned upwards.

XCIX

But it is Török who will bring the story to an end.

The description by Odoric of Pordenone speaks of a region called Reg Ruwan in the middle of the Lop desert. Now: Reg Ruwan and Lew Sha, the town on the edge of the lake Lop Nor, mean one and the same thing in different languages: *sand which flows*. It was then simply an error of translation that caused a legend to be born; it transposed the sound of a dune to the only thing that seemed comparable to it: quicksand, the dark lustre of silt. If you stumble into it, he says turning to Raoul, it will drag you down.

C

Raoul has left Elif. Not because they no longer love each other, but because they can-
not live with one another.

Something in him becomes whole, something else falls away.

Above all, with time.

There was just one further evening together in Cairo.

The needles of the tamarisk trees shining green in front of the house, the cliffs on the
bank below veined with red ore.

CI

The sandglass in the Japanese town of Nima is five metres tall, one metre wide and contains a tonne of sand that flows through a bore less than a millimetre wide.
On both of the bulbs there are markings for the months, weeks, and days. They are suspended in a system of rings vaguely reminiscent of an astrolabe.
It is said that singing dunes should be observable on other planets too, wherever there is wilderness and wind, on Mars for example, or on Venus.

Bishop's Luck, Cappaghglass, August–October 1999